Not Nice on Ice

"But I *did* sign up! I did!" Nancy cried.

Ms. Swanback shook her head. "Your name wasn't on the list, Nancy," the skating teacher said firmly.

"Now, girls," Ms. Swanback went on. "Next Saturday you should wear a skating dress and tights. Be on the rink an hour early to warm up."

Nancy wasn't listening. She stared at the list with a lump in her throat.

"I don't believe it," Nancy said to Bess. "I know my name was on the board."

"I know, too," Bess said. "Because I saw your name when I signed up. What do you think happened?"

"I think someone erased my name," Nancy said, "and put her own name in my place!"

The Nancy Drew Notebooks

Available from MINSTREL Books

For orders other than by individual consumers, Pocket Books grants a discount on the purchase of **10 or more** copies of single titles for special markets or premium use. For further details, please write to the Vice-President of Special Markets, Pocket Books, 1633 Broadway, New York, NY 10019-6785, 8th Floor.

For information on how individual consumers can place orders, please write to Mail Order Department, Simon & Schuster Inc., 200 Old Tappan Road, Old Tappan, NJ 07675.

#10

THE NANCY DREW NOTEBOOKS™

NOT NICE ON ICE

CAROLYN KEENE

Illustrated by Anthony Accardo

A MINSTREL® BOOK

Published by POCKET BOOKS
New York   London   Toronto   Sydney   Tokyo   Singapore

The sale of this book without its cover is unauthorized. If you purchased this book without a cover, you should be aware that it was reported to the publisher as "unsold and destroyed." Neither the author nor the publisher has received payment for the sale of this "stripped book."

This book is a work of fiction. Names, characters, places, and incidents are products of the author's imagination or are used fictitiously. Any resemblance to actual events or locales or persons, living or dead, is entirely coincidental.

A MINSTREL PAPERBACK *ORIGINAL*

 A Minstrel Book published by
POCKET BOOKS, a division of Simon & Schuster Inc.
1230 Avenue of the Americas, New York, NY 10020

Copyright © 1996 by Simon & Schuster Inc.
Produced by Mega-Books of New York, Inc.

All rights reserved, including the right to reproduce this book or portions thereof in any form whatsoever. For information address Pocket Books, 1230 Avenue of the Americas, New York, NY 10020

ISBN: 0-671-52711-8

First Minstrel Books printing January 1996

10 9 8 7 6 5 4 3 2

NANCY DREW, A MINSTREL BOOK and colophon are registered trademarks of Simon & Schuster Inc.

THE NANCY DREW NOTEBOOKS is a trademark of Simon & Schuster Inc.

Cover art by Aleta Jenks

Printed in the U.S.A.

1

A Skater's Dream

Watch this!" Nancy Drew called to her best friends, Bess Marvin and George Fayne.

Nancy bent forward and lifted her right leg behind her. She held her arms out for balance. Then she glided gracefully across the ice.

"You look just like Kristi Yamaguchi," Bess said.

"Do I really?" Nancy asked. She smiled. Kristi Yamaguchi was an Olympic ice-skating champion. She was coming to River Heights the next weekend as part of the Champions on Ice skating tour. Eight-year-old Nancy and Bess and George were going to see the show.

"Maybe we'll get to meet her," Nancy said as she put her right foot down. She turned to skate back to Bess and George.

Snow was falling on the pond in the park. The sky was cloudy. It was a Monday in February—a holiday. The girls had the day off from school.

Nancy pulled her fuzzy blue hat down over her ears. It matched her blue eyes. Her reddish blond hair hung out in back.

"Maybe we'll get to skate with her," Bess said. "Wouldn't that be super terrific?"

"Super impossible!" George Fayne said. George was Bess's cousin. Her real name was Georgia.

"We might get to," Bess insisted. "Our skating teacher said that we could get to help out at the ice show on Saturday."

"Help out?" George asked. "How?"

"By being flower girls," Nancy said.

2

"What's that?" George asked.

"You know," Nancy said. "People always throw flowers onto the ice at the end of an ice-skater's program. So someone has to skate out and pick up all the flowers. That's what the flower girls do."

"Sounds silly," George said.

"It's *not* silly," Bess said. "Even boys do it sometimes, but there are no boys in our skating class. Anyway, Nancy and I signed up, and we really want to do it. We're going to find out about it today."

"I still think it's silly," George said. "I mean, throwing flowers on the ice just makes a mess when the leaves fall off. Nothing like that ever happens in hockey."

Nancy laughed. "No kidding!" she said, pretending to be surprised.

"Hockey is more fun than figure skating," George said. "You get to skate really *fast* the whole time."

Just then Amara Shane came zooming across the ice. She was friends with

3

Nancy and George. They were on the same soccer team at school. She skidded to a stop in front of Bess, spraying snow and ice.

"Whoa! Look out!" Bess said. "You're getting snow on my new yellow leggings."

Amara laughed. She was wearing all blue—blue jeans, a pale blue down jacket, and a blue hat. She was covered with snow—as if she'd fallen down lots of times.

"You have snow all over you," Nancy told Amara.

"I know. I've been trying my toe loop jump," Amara said. "But I can't do it yet. I keep falling. Anyway, where's Danielle? I thought we were going to play hockey."

"We are—if Danielle ever shows up," George complained.

"She's *always* late," Amara said.

"Yeah," Bess agreed. "So if you want to play, you'll have to play without her."

"Play without her? But we need four players," Nancy said.

All at once everyone turned and stared at Bess.

"Not me," Bess said.

"Good idea!" George said, grabbing Bess's arm. "You can be on Nancy's team."

"No way!" Bess moaned, pulling back. "I'm terrible at hockey. And I don't want to get my leggings dirty."

"Oh, come on," George said. "Just until Danielle gets here."

"Please?" Nancy said.

Bess finally gave in.

"Okay," she said. "But if I fall down even once, I'm going to quit."

George and Amara quickly skated over to the edge of the pond. George picked up the hockey sticks that she and Nancy had brought. She also got an extra one for Bess. George always brought an extra stick when she played hockey. Amara picked up her stick, too.

For the next ten minutes, Nancy and Bess played hockey against George and

Amara. George and Amara scored three times. Nancy and Bess didn't score at all.

Bess hardly skated. She just carried her hockey stick around in her arms. Nancy thought Bess looked as if she didn't want to get her hockey stick dirty, either.

Finally, at about four o'clock, Danielle Margolies arrived. She was all bundled up in a pale blue parka with a hood. Underneath the hood, she had on a pale blue, brown, and white knit hat. The hat matched her hand-knit mittens.

"Where have you been?" George asked Danielle. "We were supposed to meet here at three."

"Oh, sorry," Danielle said. "I had to go shopping with my mom first."

Nancy and Bess looked at each other and rolled their eyes. Then Bess skated over to Danielle and handed her the hockey stick.

"Here," Bess said. "Take this. I'm going to practice my spins."

Nancy watched Bess skate away.

7

Then she and Danielle began playing hockey against George and Amara. Danielle played hard, but she and Nancy still lost. George was the best hockey player. It was hard to beat her.

At half-past four, Nancy saw a red minivan pull up near the pond. Bess's mother was driving. She had come to take Bess and Nancy to their skating lesson at the ice rink.

Bess skated over to Nancy.

"Time to go," Bess said.

"Do you need a ride?" Nancy called to Danielle.

"No, thanks," Danielle said. "My mom is coming back to get me."

"Then she'll be late for her lesson, too," Bess whispered under her breath.

Nancy nodded as she hurried to the edge of the pond. She put the rubber skate guards on her blades. Then she picked up her backpack and walked across the snowy ground to the car.

"I can't wait to get to the rink," Nancy said as she climbed into the car. "We're going to be flower girls—I hope." Then she added, "Hi, Mrs. Marvin."

"Hello, Nancy," Bess's mother said. She gave Nancy a sweet smile. Nancy liked Mrs. Marvin. She had blond hair and pink cheeks, just like Bess.

It took only a few minutes to drive to the rink. When they arrived, Nancy and Bess hopped out of the minivan. Nancy grabbed her backpack from the floor in the backseat. It had her regular shoes in it. Bess took her bag with her shoes, too.

"See you at six," Mrs. Marvin called.

Nancy and Bess waved goodbye. Then they hurried inside. The lobby of the ice rink was large. On the left was a door to the girls' locker room. Right next to it was the boys' locker room.

At the other end of the lobby was a place to rent skates and a snack bar. Next to the skate rental counter was a red door leading into the ice rink.

But Nancy and Bess almost never went through the red door. Instead, they hurried into the girls' locker room. They put their jackets, backpacks, and shoes in empty lockers. Then they walked through a green swinging door that led straight from the locker room into the ice rink.

Inside, the ice rink was dark. Straight ahead was the narrow end of the oval ice rink. On the two long sides of the ice were wooden bleachers. The open floor space between the locker room and the ice was covered with black rubber mats. That way, the skaters could walk to the ice in their skates without scratching the blades.

The ice itself was circled by a low wooden wall. It was called "the boards." There were only two openings in the boards—one on each side.

A lot of girls were already on the ice when Nancy arrived. So was Claire Swanback, the skating teacher.

Nancy and Bess hurried onto the ice and skated toward their teacher.

"Girls," Ms. Swanback called. "Gather around. I have an announcement to make."

"This is it," Nancy said, grabbing

Bess's arm. "She's going to tell us about being flower girls."

"Don't hold on to me," Bess said. "I'll fall."

Nancy skated a little closer to the teacher. Ms. Swanback had a piece of paper in her hands.

"Well, I have good news," Ms. Swanback said. "I wasn't sure how many flower girls we needed. But the ice show people called me. They said that all ten girls who signed up will get to be flower girls for the show."

"Yay!" Nancy and Bess both cheered.

"Shh," Ms. Swanback said, putting a finger to her lips. "Let me read the names, just to be sure you all still want to do it."

Nancy clapped her hands together. Of course I still want to do it! she thought.

Ms. Swanback started to read aloud. "Rebecca, Laura, Mandy, Danielle, Megan, Susan . . ."

Hey, where's my name? Nancy wondered.

". . . Amara, Bess, Molly, and Julie,"
Ms. Swanback said.

"What about me?" Nancy called out.

"I'm sorry," Ms. Swanback said.
"But I guess you forgot to sign up in
time. Your name wasn't on the list."

2

Not Fair

But I *did* sign up! I did!" Nancy cried.

Ms. Swanback shook her head. "Your name wasn't on the list, Nancy," the teacher said firmly.

"But I know I signed up," Nancy said again. "I put my name on that white board in the lobby. I used the blue marker that was hanging there."

Ms. Swanback pushed her long brown hair away from her face. Then she looked at Nancy thoughtfully.

"Nancy, there were only ten spaces on the board," Ms. Swanback said. "All ten spaces were full when I took the board down today. And your name wasn't on the list. I erased the board, but I copied the names onto this piece of paper, exactly as they were. Here—you can see for yourself."

Ms. Swanback handed the list to Nancy.

"Now, girls," Ms. Swanback went on. "I want to tell you about next Saturday. You should wear a skating dress and tights. Be at the rink at four o'clock to watch the champion skaters warm up . . ."

Nancy wasn't listening. She stared at the list with a lump in her throat.

"I don't believe it," Nancy said to Bess. "I know my name was on the board."

"I know, too," Bess said. "Because I saw your name when I signed up. What do you think happened?"

"I think someone erased my name," Nancy said, "and put her own name in my place. And it's not fair!"

A few girls looked over at Nancy. They had heard what she'd said, and they looked as if they felt sorry for her.

Bess nodded. "That's so terrible," she said. "Who do you think did it?"

"I don't know," Nancy said, lowering her voice so the other girls couldn't hear. "But I'm going to find out. If I could remember where my name was on the list—I mean, which number—then I'd know who did it."

"Think hard," Bess said. "You're good at figuring things out. If you can prove who did it, maybe Ms. Swanback will let you be a flower girl."

Nancy closed her eyes and thought. She could picture everything perfectly: The shiny white board hanging in the lobby. The blue marker dangling on a string. And the names.

There had already been a few names on the list when Nancy had written her own. But how many?

"I think I was somewhere in the middle," Nancy said, opening her eyes. "Maybe number three, four, or five."

Bess grabbed the list from Nancy's hand. "Okay, let's see. Number three is Mandy Trout. Number four is Danielle.

15

And five is Megan Kline. So those are your suspects."

"Yes," Nancy said. "And maybe even number six. My name could have been that far down on the list."

"That's Susan Hong's name," Bess said. "Put her on the suspect list, too."

"I will," Nancy said, starting to skate away.

"Hey, where are you going?" Bess called.

Nancy didn't answer. All she said was, "I'll be right back."

She hurried into the locker room with Ms. Swanback's list of names still in her hand.

I've got to write these clues down, Nancy thought. Before I forget.

The floor in the locker room was covered with thick rubber mats, too. That way Nancy didn't have to take off her skates or put on her skate guards. She went right to the locker where she had put her things.

Inside was her backpack. And inside her backpack was her special blue

16

notebook. She always used it when she was trying to solve a mystery.

Nancy took it out and sat down on a long wooden bench.

At the top of a new page, she wrote: "The Ice-Skating Mystery."

Below that, she wrote: "Ms. Swanback's list.

"1. Rebecca 2. Laura 3. Mandy 4. Danielle 5. Megan 6. Susan 7. Amara 8. Bess 9. Molly 10. Julie."

Then she wrote: "Suspects: Mandy, Danielle, Megan, and Susan."

"What are you doing?" a voice suddenly said.

Nancy was startled. She looked up. Danielle had just walked in. She was late for her lesson, as usual.

"Oh—hi," Nancy said. "I was just writing something."

"In your detective's notebook?" Danielle asked.

"Yes," Nancy said, closing it quickly.

"Can I see?" Danielle asked.

"No," Nancy said. "It's private."

"Oh," Danielle said. She tossed her

long blond braid over her shoulders and gave Nancy a hurt look.

"Come on," Nancy said as she put the notebook back in her locker. "We're missing the lesson."

Nancy hopped up and headed toward the green swinging door. It led right into the ice rink. Danielle sat down to put on her skates.

"Oh, by the way," Nancy said. "Ms. Swanback announced your name. You get to be one of the flower girls for the ice show."

Nancy watched Danielle's face carefully. But the lights in the locker room were dim. She couldn't tell if Danielle blushed or looked guilty.

"Great!" Danielle said. "That will be so much fun!"

Then Danielle finished tying her skates. She hurried toward the ice. Nancy followed her. But just as Nancy stepped onto the ice, Bess came skating up.

"Nancy!" Bess said, grabbing Nancy's arm. "Guess what I just remembered?"

"What?" Nancy asked.

"I think I know who did it!" Bess said. "I know who erased your name from the list!"

3

Clues on the Ice

Who?" Nancy asked, staring wide-eyed at Bess.

"It was Susan Hong," Bess announced as she and Nancy stood near the opening in the boards that surrounded the ice rink.

"How do you know?" Nancy asked.

"Because I saw her. I mean, I just remembered that I saw her erasing her *own* name from the board, anyway," Bess said.

"Really?"

"Yes," Bess said. "It was last Saturday. George and I were here to skate. I saw Susan in the lobby. She had a tissue in her hand, and she was wiping her name off the board."

"Hmmm," Nancy said. "That's weird."

"I know," Bess said. "I mean, why would she erase her own name?"

"I don't know," Nancy said. "And anyway, her name is back *on* the list. Ms. Swanback said so. She's one of the flower girls."

"Oh, yeah," Bess said, looking puzzled. "Well, do you think maybe she erased your name, too?"

Nancy shook her head. "I don't know. Why would she, if she was erasing her own name?"

"Good question," Bess admitted. "But I'll tell you one thing. While you were in the locker room I talked to Ms. Swanback. I don't think she believed you—about writing your name on the list. But she said that if you can prove someone erased your name, she'll let you be a flower girl."

"Good," Nancy said. "Then I'll have

to work fast. Come on—we're missing the lesson."

Nancy and Bess both skated over to Ms. Swanback. She was teaching everyone how to skate backward.

Nancy took her place in the group, and listened carefully to Ms. Swanback's instructions. Nancy was good at the basics. She could skate forward and backward on two feet. She could skate forward on one foot. And she could spin in a circle.

But she couldn't skate backward using only one foot at a time. She definitely couldn't do the crossover strokes. Those were the hardest—the ones where she had to lift one foot and cross it over the other.

Ms. Swanback showed Nancy how to glide backward on one skate. It was easier when the teacher was helping her.

Then Nancy practiced on her own.

"Keep your weight centered over your skating foot," Amara called out to Nancy.

"I'm trying!" Nancy cried. She giggled as her foot wobbled and she almost fell down.

Meanwhile Ms. Swanback worked with the other girls. Some of them were better skaters than Nancy.

Finally the lesson was over. Everyone had to leave the ice. Then the big Zamboni machine came out. It looked like a huge motorized lawn mower. It scraped the ice, leaving it perfectly smooth and clean.

Nancy and Bess hurried into the locker room to change out of their skates.

"Let's leave our things in our lockers," Bess said. "It's only a quarter to six, and my mom won't be here until six o'clock. She gave me some money. She said we could go to the snack bar and get hot chocolate."

"Great!" Nancy said.

Nancy stuffed her skates into her locker. But she didn't lock it. She and her friends didn't use locks. It was too hard to remember the combinations.

Then Nancy and Bess went out to the lobby. The snack bar was just a small window with a counter. Bess ordered the hot chocolate. She and Nancy sat at a nearby table to drink it.

As they sat, they watched people leaving the rink. One by one, the other girls from Nancy's class came out of the locker room.

"See you tomorrow at school," Amara called to Nancy and Bess.

"Bye," Nancy called back.

Pretty soon the rink was almost empty. Nearly everyone had gone home. The rink always closed early on Monday nights.

"I can't drink this hot chocolate," Bess said, blowing on it. "It's too hot."

"Me, either," Nancy said. "I already burned my tongue."

"Come on," Bess said. "We'd better get our skates and wait by the front door. My mom will be here soon."

Nancy and Bess dumped their cups of hot chocolate in the trash. They headed toward the locker room again.

Nancy pushed open the locker room door. There were two long rows of lockers in the middle of the room, and lockers on the side walls.

At first the room looked empty to Nancy. But as she went around the corner of one row of lockers, she thought she heard footsteps running away.

"Who's there?" Nancy called.

No one answered. Then she heard the big green door to the ice rink open and close.

"Who was that?" Bess said.

"I don't know," Nancy said. "But look. My locker's open. Someone's been snooping in here!"

Bess's eyes grew wide. "I don't believe it!" she said. "Is anything missing?"

Nancy checked inside the locker. "No. But I think someone was reading my notebook. Look."

She pointed to her special blue notebook. It was sticking halfway out of her backpack.

Nancy ran toward the green door and

opened it. Bess was right behind her. They stepped into the dark ice rink.

The rink was darker than usual. It was almost spooky. Only two small lights shone overhead. Nancy looked around quickly. No one seemed to be there.

"Where did she go?" Bess wondered, looking all around. Her voice echoed in the empty rink.

"I don't know. Maybe back to the lobby, through the red door," Nancy said, pointing.

She hurried over to the red door at the other side of the rink. It was the one that led straight back into the lobby.

"We have to catch her," Bess said. She was right behind Nancy.

Nancy yanked open the door to the lobby. She stuck her head out to see if anyone was there. But no one was.

Bess put her hands on her hips.

"You don't think she went into the *boys'* locker room, do you?" she said.

Nancy glanced toward the boys'

locker-room door. "No," she said, shaking her head.

"Well, she got away—whoever she was," Bess said.

Nancy nodded. But she was staring past Bess, at the ice.

"Look," Nancy said. She pointed. "I think she left us a clue."

"Where?" Bess asked, turning to see where Nancy was pointing.

"On the ice," Nancy said. "See those lines? Someone was skating after the Zamboni cleaned it."

Nancy hurried over toward the ice and looked at it carefully. "Someone was practicing a three-turn," she said. "You can tell because that line looks like the number three."

"That's what Danielle was working on today!" Bess exclaimed. "She's the only one in our class who can do a three-turn."

"Exactly," Nancy said. "She must have stayed late, after the Zamboni guy was done. Then she got back on the ice."

"So you think she was snooping in your locker, too?" Bess asked.

Nancy shrugged. "I don't know for sure," she said. "But she could have been. She saw me writing in my notebook. She asked to see it."

"Oh, wow," Bess said. "Then I'll bet she's the one who erased your name from the board, too."

"Maybe," Nancy said as she headed back toward the locker-room door. "But we've got to get proof."

Nancy reached for the door handle. She pulled hard, but it wouldn't open.

"Oh, no," Nancy said. "It's locked. We're locked in!"

4

Trapped!

"Help!" Bess cried. "Let us out! Help!"

Nancy didn't want to scream. She wasn't *that* scared. But she *did* want to get out of the ice rink. It wasn't fun being locked up in the dark.

She ran to the red door—the one that led into the lobby. But now it was locked, too.

"Let us out!" Bess yelled.

Nancy hurried back to the locker-room door and pounded on it with her fist. "Hello?" Nancy called. "Is anyone there? Hello! We're trapped in here! Let us out!"

Then Nancy stopped pounding and

listened. "Shh," she told Bess. "I hear someone moving around inside the locker room."

Bess held her breath and listened, too.

"Maybe it's Danielle," Bess whispered. "Maybe she's trying to trap us in here, just to be mean."

Just then the door to the locker room opened. A beam of light streamed into the dark ice rink. Nancy saw a man standing in the doorway. With the light behind him, it was hard to see his face.

"What happened? You girls get locked inside?" the man said.

Nancy recognized his voice. It was Mr. Radnor, the ice rink manager.

"Yes," Nancy said.

Mr. Radnor flipped a switch near the door. Some of the lights came back on.

"Sorry about that," he said. "I thought everyone was gone, so I locked these doors a few minutes early. I've been cleaning up the lobby. Sorry if I gave you a scare."

"Oh, we weren't scared," Bess said

quickly. She shook her head hard, and her long blond hair bounced.

Nancy burst out laughing. "*Who* wasn't scared?" Nancy said. "You sounded pretty scared to me."

"Never mind," Bess said, sticking her nose in the air. "Come on. My mom is probably waiting in the parking lot."

Nancy hurried to get her backpack. Then she and Bess walked to the front door. Mrs. Marvin was parked right outside, just as Bess thought.

Nancy and Bess got into the red minivan. Then Nancy took her blue notebook out of her backpack again. She opened it to the page where she had written "The Ice-Skating Mystery."

"Danielle," she wrote. "Snooping in my notebook. Why?"

Then Nancy closed her notebook and put it back into her pack. She folded her arms across her chest.

I've got to find out who took my name off the list before Saturday, she thought. And that means I have less than a week!

"Nancy! Over here!" a voice called.

Nancy looked across the school playground. It was recess the next day. Through the falling snowflakes, Nancy saw Bess and George waving. They were all the way across the playground. George was lying on her back, making a snow angel.

Nancy ran to join her friends.

"Brrr, it's so cold," Bess said, shivering.

"I'm not cold," Nancy said. "I love it!"

She turned around and stood with her back to a clean spot of snow. Then she stretched her arms out wide.

"Timmmm-berrr!" George shouted as Nancy fell straight back into the snow.

Nancy lay on her back for a moment and opened her mouth. She let the snowflakes fall onto her tongue.

"They don't taste as cold as you think they will," Nancy announced.

George stood up from her snow angel and stepped away carefully.

"Your turn," she said to her cousin Bess.

"No, thanks," Bess said. "I don't want to get my new coat snowy."

"You and your clothes," George said, rolling her eyes. "Do you have *any* clothes that you can actually *play* in?"

"Sure," Bess said. "My old clothes. But I never wear them."

"Why not?" Nancy asked, still lying on her back in the snow.

"Because they're old, silly!" Bess said. "I like my new clothes better."

Nancy got up and brushed off her own coat. Then she looked around the playground. She had been looking for Danielle Margolies all through lunchtime. Danielle was in a different third-grade class.

"If you're looking for Danielle, she's not here," George said. "Amara told me. Danielle's sick today."

"Oh," Nancy said.

"But we could spy on your other suspects," George suggested. Nancy and Bess had told George all about the mystery. "Who else is on the list?"

"Mandy Trout and Megan," Nancy said. "And maybe Susan Hong."

"Well, there's Mandy now," George said.

Nancy followed George's gaze. George was right—Mandy was walking toward the school door. Nancy knew it was her, because she always wore her scarf wrapped around her mouth.

"Where's she going?" Nancy wondered out loud. "We're not supposed to go back inside until the bell rings."

"I'll bet she's up to something," Bess said, pulling Nancy by the sleeve. "Let's follow her."

Nancy hurried toward the school. She didn't need Bess to pull her. She wanted to solve this mystery more than anything in the world.

"Wait," George said. "She's turning around."

All three girls stopped and pretended to be talking to each other. But Nancy watched Mandy out of the corner of her eye. Mandy seemed to be checking to make sure no one saw her. Then she slipped inside the school building.

Nancy, Bess, and George followed. But they didn't get too close. They didn't want her to see them.

The halls were empty. Mandy hurried to her classroom—Mrs. Keller's room— and sneaked inside.

The three friends waited until Mandy had closed the door from inside the room.

Then they tiptoed up to the door. Nancy peeked through the glass pane to see what Mandy was doing. Bess and George stayed close to the wall, out of sight.

"What's she doing?" Bess whispered in Nancy's ear.

Nancy shook her head. She didn't know the answer yet. Mandy was walking toward the blackboard. She had an eraser in her hand.

"What's she doing?" Bess repeated.

"Oh, no!" Nancy gasped. "There's a list of classroom chores on the blackboard."

"So what?" George said softly.

"So she's erasing her name from the list," Nancy said. "And she's writing in someone else's name instead!"

5

I Hate You, Nancy Drew

Quickly Nancy pulled open the door
to the classroom and stepped in.

Mandy jumped. She turned from the
blackboard with the chalk and eraser
still in her hands.

"Nancy!" Mandy cried out. "You
scared me!"

Bess and George followed Nancy into
the room.

"What are you doing?" Nancy asked
Mandy.

"Nothing," Mandy said, her face
turning bright red. Quickly she put the
chalk down on the blackboard tray.
But she still held on to the eraser.

"That's not true," Nancy said. "I saw

you. You erased your name from that chores list on the blackboard."

"What were *you* doing? Spying on me?" Mandy said.

"You're not supposed to be in here during lunch," Bess said in an accusing tone of voice.

"Neither are you," Mandy said back.

Nancy folded her arms. "Look," she said. "Maybe I was spying on you. But I have a reason. I'm trying to find out who erased my name from the sign-up board at the ice rink. Because *someone* did. And I just saw you doing the exact same thing."

Mandy's face turned twice as red. Tears filled her eyes.

"I hate you, Nancy Drew!" she cried. Then she threw the eraser down on the floor and ran out of the room.

For a minute Bess and George were silent. They looked at Nancy, waiting to see what she would say.

"I didn't mean to make her cry," Nancy said slowly.

"I know," Bess said. "But she cries

all the time. Anyway, at least you caught her. She's probably the one who erased your name at the ice rink. And now *she'll* get to be a flower girl and you won't!"

"It's not fair," George said.

No, it's not, Nancy thought. She was so mad, she felt her face getting hot.

"But what about Danielle?" George said to Nancy. "I thought you told me *she* was the one who snooped in your locker at the rink."

"Oh, yeah. That's right," Bess said. "Now I'm all mixed up. That means Danielle and Mandy are *both* still suspects."

Nancy was mixed up, too. But that didn't worry her very much. She knew it was just part of being a detective. It was hard to solve mysteries.

Just then the bell rang. Lunch was over.

"Anyway, it's better to have too many clues than too few," Nancy said as she and her friends hurried back to class.

*   *   *

By Friday after school, Nancy was very worried.

"Tomorrow is the ice show," Nancy said to Bess. "I've got to solve this mystery soon, or I won't get to be a flower girl."

"I feel so bad," Bess said. "It won't be any fun for me to be one, if you can't."

The two of them had just arrived at the skating pond in the park. Nancy sat down on a snowy log near the pond to put on her skates. Bess did the same thing. They left their boots by the log. Then they skated out onto the ice.

"Have you figured out who did it?" Bess asked as they twirled in fast circles.

Nancy shook her head. "Not yet. But I've narrowed it down to three. Mandy Trout, Danielle Margolies, and Susan Hong."

"Big deal," Bess said. "Those were the only suspects you had in the first place."

"No," Nancy said. "I also had Megan's name on the list. Remember? But that was just because of where her name was on the sign-up board. And she hasn't acted guilty or done anything suspicious all week. So I decided she wasn't a real suspect. I crossed her off the list last night."

Nancy skated away from Bess and did a quick spin. She was wearing one of her favorite outdoor ice-skating outfits—blue jeans and a thick red-and-white sweater. The sweater had a snowflake pattern knitted into it. Nancy also wore red-and-white snowflake mittens, and a red scarf.

The scarf twirled around as Nancy spun on the ice.

"Hey, look. There's Susan Hong," Bess said. "She's practicing her toe loop jump."

Nancy skidded to a stop and watched as the other girl skated backward on her right skate. Then Susan reached her left foot back and tapped the toe pick on the front of the blade into the ice. An instant later she jumped into the air and turned around. She landed perfectly on her right skate again.

"She's such a good skater," Bess said. "I'll bet she'll be an Olympic champion someday."

"I wish I could do that jump," Nancy said.

Then she looked around at the pond. A bunch of teenagers were playing hockey at one end. Two grown-ups were skating together near the banks of the pond. And a lot of girls from Nancy's skating class were practicing their figure skating in groups of two or three.

Mandy Trout was one of them. She was all by herself at the far end of the pond. Her scarf was over her mouth, as usual. She kept falling down.

"There's Mandy," Bess said.

"I know," Nancy said. "But she's avoiding us. Every time I skate up to her, she skates away."

"Let's pretend we're flower girls," Bess said. "I'll throw some sticks on the ice, and you skate out and pick them up. Pretend that they're flowers."

Nancy swallowed hard. I hope I get to be a flower girl, she thought. But what were the chances? Time was running out.

For the next half hour, Nancy and Bess practiced picking up "flowers" and skating away with them. It was fun. But it made Nancy feel bad, too.

Finally it was half past four—time to go home. Nancy and Bess were both cold.

They skated over to the log and changed out of their skates. Then they got up to leave.

But just as Nancy was walking away from the pond, she heard a small voice calling her name.

Nancy turned around and saw Mandy Trout running toward her.

"Wait!" Mandy called. "Don't leave. I have to tell you the truth!"

6

Mandy's Confession

Nancy stared at Mandy.

"The truth?" Nancy said. "About what?"

Mandy gulped. "It's about the other day at school," Mandy said. "When I erased my name from the chores list on the blackboard."

"Oh," Nancy said. She nodded and held her breath. Was Mandy going to admit that she had erased Nancy's name at the skating rink, too?

"I did it for a reason," Mandy explained. "See, I was supposed to clean out the hamster cage that day at school. But I hate that job."

"Me, too," Bess said, jumping into

the conversation. She made a face. "It's yucky."

"Shh," Nancy said. She nudged Bess to be quiet.

"Anyway, I overheard you talking about how someone erased your name at the ice rink," Mandy went on. "So I got the idea to do the same thing at school. I took my name off the chores list. Then I wrote Bobby Mercado's name on the list instead."

"Oh," Nancy said.

"That wasn't right," Bess said firmly. But then she added, "I don't blame you, though. Hamsters are icky."

"I printed Bobby's name just like Mrs. Keller does," Mandy said proudly.

"But what about at the skating rink?" Nancy asked quickly.

"I didn't do that. *Honest* I didn't," Mandy said. "I just heard you talking about it. So I decided to be a copycat."

Nancy's face fell. She was disappointed. She wanted to solve this mystery—today!—so she could be a flower girl tomorrow.

"Anyway, I just wanted you to know," Mandy went on. "After you caught me, I felt really bad. So after lunch I put my name *back* on the chores list."

"Eww," Bess said. "Poor you. Was the hamster cage gross?"

"Totally," Mandy said. She gave Bess a grateful smile, and both girls giggled.

"Well, thanks for telling me," Nancy said. But she still felt bad about not solving the mystery. "I believe you."

Mandy looked so happy and relieved. "I really hope you get to be a flower girl," Mandy said. "You're such a good skater. You and Bess are both better than me."

That was true, Nancy thought. But she didn't say so.

"Well, I'll see you tomorrow at the ice show," Nancy said. "I guess I'll go with George and watch the show from the seats."

"Yeah," Mandy said. "I'll wave to you, if that will help."

"Thanks," Nancy said as she turned

away. But she knew it wouldn't help. Nothing would help. It just wasn't fair to be cheated out of a chance to skate with all the Olympic stars.

Nancy stomped her feet in the snow and started up the bank again. The sky was turning gray. It would be dark soon. She and Bess were not allowed to be out when it was getting dark.

"We'd better hurry," Nancy said to Bess.

But just then she passed the logs where everyone sat to change their skates. Nancy looked down and saw something lying in the snow.

"Hey, look," Nancy said, bending down.

She picked up a hand-knit wool mitten. It had patterns of pale blue, brown, and white.

"I know whose that is," Bess said. "It's Danielle's. Her grandmother made those mittens for her."

Bess glanced around the pond. "Danielle's not here," she announced. "I saw her before, but she's gone now."

"Hmmm," Nancy said, studying the

mitten closely. "There's a dark blue smudge on the white part of the fingertips. I wonder what it is?"

"Dirt?" Bess asked.

"I don't think so," Nancy said. "It doesn't look like dirt to me."

"Oh, well," Bess said. "Let's take it home and give it to her tomorrow."

"Okay," Nancy said, putting the mitten in her jacket pocket. "Or maybe I'll call her about it tonight."

When Nancy got home, she hurried into the kitchen to get warm. Hannah Gruen, the Drew family housekeeper, was making dinner. She gave Nancy a taste of some warm potato soup that was on the stove.

Then Nancy remembered the mitten. She reached for the phone. She dialed Danielle's number.

"Hello?" a girl's voice said. It sounded like Danielle's older sister, Marlo.

"Hello," Nancy said. "This is Nancy Drew. May I please speak to Danielle?"

"Oh, hi, Nancy," the older girl said. "This is Marlo. She's not here right now."

"Oh," Nancy said.

"She went out to buy a new skating dress," Marlo went on. "To wear at the ice show tomorrow. She's a flower girl. Are you?"

Nancy felt a lump forming in her throat. "No," she managed to say. "I'm not."

"Oh, too bad," Marlo said. "It sounds like lots of fun. All kinds of champions are going to be there, you know."

Nancy wanted to cry. "I know," she said. She could hardly talk. "Well, tell Danielle I found her mitten. Tell her I'll give it to her tomorrow."

Then Nancy hung up the phone with a bang. Tears filled her eyes.

"I'll give it to her tomorrow," Nancy repeated, even though no one was listening. "Tomorrow—when she's a flower girl at the ice show and I'm not!"

7

The Too-Late Truth

Cheer up, Pudding Pie," Nancy's father said as he drove her to the ice rink. It was almost four o'clock on Saturday afternoon.

Nancy didn't answer. She just stared out the window and felt glum.

"At least you're going to *see* all the famous skaters," Carson Drew said. "You'll even get to watch them rehearse. That's pretty special."

"I know," Nancy said. "But it isn't fair. I signed up to be a flower girl. I should get to be one."

"I know," Carson Drew said. "But life isn't always fair, Nancy. I'm sorry, but that's the truth."

Nancy thought about that. She knew her father was right. But she still felt bad.

"Mostly I'm upset because I can't figure out who did it," Nancy said.

Carson Drew smiled. "Well, maybe there's still time," he said. "Just remember what I've always told you. Don't get confused by the clues. Just think clearly and decide what *really* makes sense."

Nancy looked down at the mitten she had found at the pond. Danielle's mitten.

You make it sound so easy, Dad, Nancy thought. But it's not.

Just then they arrived at the skating rink. Nancy saw a big truck parked in the parking lot. It said Champions on Ice Tour on the side.

"I'll bet the costumes are in there," her father said.

Nancy's face lit up. This *was* going to be fun, even if she didn't get to be a flower girl! Quickly she hopped out of the car.

"I'll meet you in the lobby at six o'clock, right before the show," Carson Drew called.

"Okay, Daddy," Nancy said, waving as she ran into the building.

Inside, the doors to the rink were closed. Most people weren't allowed to watch the skaters rehearse. But Ms. Swanback was standing there. She let Nancy and her other students go in.

Nancy found Bess and George already seated. Amara was in the row behind them. So were some of the other girls. But the figure skaters weren't on the ice yet.

"Hi," Nancy said to her friends. Then Nancy looked at George with a strange expression. "But why are *you* here?" she asked George. "You're not in our skating class."

"Ms. Swanback let me in early," George said. "I'm here to watch the River Heights hockey team. They're going to practice at five, right after the figure skaters warm up."

"Oh," Nancy said, nodding.

George leaned over toward Nancy. "Have you figured it out yet? About the sign-up board?" she asked.

"No," Nancy said, shaking her head.

"Oh, well," George said. "Maybe someone won't show up, Maybe you'll get to be a flower girl anyway."

"Yeah," Bess said. "Like Danielle. She's always late. Maybe she'll be late again."

Nancy glanced around. Danielle wasn't there yet—Bess was right. Danielle *was* late.

"But I don't have my skating dress with me," Nancy said.

"Oh, right," Bess said.

All at once the lights in the rink went out. Then a beautiful pink spotlight swept across the ice. Music began to play on the speaker system.

Then Nancy saw her. Kristi Yamaguchi! She skated out onto the ice in her gold-and-silver skating dress. She was the most beautiful skater Nancy had ever seen.

A few minutes later, the other champion skaters rushed onto the ice, too. They all began to practice their spins and jumps.

"Aren't they great?" Bess said, her voice high.

"They're the best," Nancy said. "But there are so many of them! I don't know which one to watch."

"I like the guy who's dressed up like a cat," George said. "His jumps are amazing. He'd be a great hockey player!"

Nancy nodded and stared. It was the most exciting show she had ever seen, and this was only the rehearsal! She could hardly wait until the real show that night.

For the next hour, Nancy watched the skaters. Then the figure skating rehearsal was over. The Zamboni machine came out to clean the ice.

Then the hockey team arrived to practice.

"Remember, you promised to stay and watch the hockey practice, too,"

George said. "I want to see the new goalie. He just moved to our block."

"Hockey is so boring," Bess said, standing up. "I'm going to get hot chocolate in the lobby."

"You mean you're going to go burn your tongue," George teased.

Bess laughed. "Yeah, probably," she said.

"That's okay," George said. "Nancy will stay here with me. Won't you, Nancy?"

Nancy nodded and settled back in her seat to watch. But her head was spinning. So many skaters! It was hard to keep track of what was happening in the practice game.

Suddenly Nancy noticed a balding man in a white shirt. He was standing near the edge of the ice rink. He had a small white erasable board in his hands. With a marker, he was drawing X's and lines on the board.

Nancy perked up. "What's that man doing?" she asked George.

"He's the hockey coach," George

said. "He's drawing pictures of the hockey plays."

Nancy stared at him for several minutes. He was using an erasable marker on a shiny white board. First he drew some X's and O's. Then he drew lines. He showed the drawing to his players.

Then he took a white handkerchief and used it to erase the marks.

"Look at his handkerchief," Nancy said to George. "It's getting all smudged with blue ink."

"Oh, give me a break," George said. "You sound as bad as Bess—worrying about everything getting dirty."

"No," Nancy said. "That's not what I mean. I mean it reminds me of something else."

"What?" George asked.

Nancy stared a minute longer. Then all at once her face lit up. "I know!" Nancy said. "That's the same kind of dark blue smudge as the one on Danielle's mitten!"

Nice in the End

What mitten?" George asked. She looked puzzled.

"This one," Nancy said. She reached in her pocket and took out Danielle's mitten. She held it up as if it were a prize fish she had just caught.

"That's Danielle's?" George asked. "But where did you get it?"

"I found it at the skating pond," Nancy said. "And look. It has a dark blue smudge on the fingertips. Just like on the coach's handkerchief."

"So?" George still looked puzzled.

"So I think I know how the smudge got there," Nancy said. "I think it's ink. I think Danielle used her mitten to erase my name from the sign-up board in the lobby."

George's mouth fell open. Her eyes grew big. "I'll bet you're right," she said.

"I wish she'd hurry up and get here," Nancy said, glancing all around.

"She's here," George said, pointing. "Didn't you see her? She's been sitting on the other side of the ice rink this whole time."

"Thanks," Nancy said. She jumped up and hurried to the other side of the skating rink. She walked up to Danielle with the mitten in her hand.

"Oh, hi," Danielle said nervously. "You found my mitten."

"Yes," Nancy said. "But I have something to ask you. It's about this smudge—this *blue ink* smudge."

Danielle's face turned red. She looked away.

"It looks as if you used your mitten to erase some ink from one of those white boards," Nancy went on. "Like

64

the one in the lobby. The sign-up board."

Danielle stared at the mitten for a moment without looking up. Then she started to nod slowly.

"I'm really, really sorry," she said quickly. "I did it. I erased your name. It's just that I was late to my lesson that day—the day Ms. Swanback put up the sign. By the time I got there, all the spaces were full."

"So you rubbed off my name and put in your own?" Nancy asked. Even though she knew it was true, she still couldn't believe someone would do something like that.

"Yes," Danielle admitted.

"And then you snooped in my locker?" Nancy went on.

"Yes," Danielle said. "I saw you writing in that detective's notebook of yours. I wanted to see if you suspected me."

"I did," Nancy said.

"I know," Danielle said, blushing some more. She looked very unhappy.

"Please don't be mad at me. I'll go tell Ms. Swanback the truth right now. She's in the locker room."

"Okay," Nancy agreed. She tried to smile at Danielle. "At least you told me the truth."

With the mitten still in her hand, Danielle led the way to Ms. Swanback. She quickly told the teacher the whole story.

"Oh, I'm so sorry," Ms. Swanback said to Nancy.

Nancy nodded. "I know. I was really mad at Danielle. But it's okay now."

"I'm disappointed in you, Danielle," Ms. Swanback said. Then she turned to Nancy. "But I'm sorry about how I acted, too. I didn't believe you when you told me you were on the list."

Nancy nodded again. "I know."

"I'm really sorry," Ms. Swanback repeated. "Of course you can skate tonight instead of Danielle. And, Danielle, you can take Nancy's seat in the stands. You can just sit and watch the skating show. Now hurry up and get changed, Nancy," Ms. Swanback went on. "I want the flower girls to warm up on the ice before the show starts."

"But my costume! And my skates!" Nancy said. "I don't have them with me!"

"Oh, dear," Ms. Swanback said. "Can you call your father and ask him to bring them?"

Nancy looked at her watch. "He's supposed to be here right now," she said. "It's probably too late."

Nancy's eyes started to fill up with tears. This just wasn't fair! She had solved the mystery, but she still couldn't skate.

Then all of a sudden Nancy felt someone tapping her on the shoulder.

"You can wear my new skating dress," Danielle said softly. "And my skates, if they fit you."

"Really?" Nancy said. "That's great!"

"Why, that's very nice of you, Danielle," Ms. Swanback said.

The teacher eyed Danielle for a minute. "I'll tell you what," Ms. Swanback said to Danielle. "How would you like to stay behind the boards with me during the show? We can watch from the sidelines. And then you can help the other girls carry the flowers to the skaters after the show is over."

"Oh, that would be wonderful," Danielle said. "Thanks! Thanks a lot."

Nancy was so excited, she didn't know what to do first. She ran to the lobby to meet her father and tell him what had happened. Then she hurried to the locker room to meet Bess.

As fast as she could, she told Bess the whole story.

"But what about Susan Hong?" Bess blurted out.

"I don't know," Nancy said.

"What about me?" a voice on the other side of the row of lockers said. Then Susan came around the corner.

Bess blushed, but Nancy smiled. "We were just wondering something," Nancy said. "Why did you erase your name from the sign-up board? And then how did your name get put back on the list?"

"My mother signed me up again," Susan answered shyly. "I didn't want to skate in front of so many people, but she said I had to."

"But why didn't you want to?" Nancy asked.

"You're such a good skater!" Bess exclaimed.

"Thanks," Susan said. "I just get scared when a lot of people are watching."

"Don't be scared," Nancy said. "You can hang out with us. We'll stick together."

"Yeah," Bess said. Then she lowered her voice to a whisper. "And don't worry," she added. "No one will notice you. They'll all be watching Mandy. She falls down so much."

Nancy, Bess, and Susan giggled quietly. They didn't want Mandy to hear them. They didn't want to hurt her feelings.

"We'd better get ready," Bess said as she hurried back to her locker.

"Okay," Nancy said. Her eyes were twinkling with excitement.

Within a few minutes, the ice show started. The first skaters were the Russian pairs champions. All the flower girls watched from behind the boards.

As soon as the act was over, Ms. Swanback sent Nancy, Bess, and Susan onto the ice. They skated around the huge oval, picking up all the flowers that the fans had thrown.

Nancy loved the feeling of skating in front of such a big crowd.

"That was so cool!" Susan said when they were done.

"I know," Nancy said, smiling. "That was the most fun!"

Then Nancy looked down at her skating dress, the one Danielle had loaned her. It was blue satin with silver trim. The silver trim glittered under the bright lights on the ice.

It was so *nice* of Danielle to let me wear her dress, Nancy thought.

Nancy turned and started walking toward the locker room.

"Where are you going?" Bess called.

"I just have to write something down," Nancy called. "I'll be right back."

In the locker room, Nancy reached into her locker and took out her blue notebook. She opened it to the next blank page. Then she wrote:

Today I solved The Ice-Skating Mystery. I learned that sometimes a person can be not nice one day. And then a day later, they can be nice again. *Very* nice!

Case closed.

**Join eight-year old Nancy and her best friends
as they collect clues and solve mysteries in**

THE NANCY DREW NOTEBOOKS®

#1: THE SLUMBER PARTY SECRET 87945-6/$3.50
#2: THE LOST LOCKET 87946-4/$3.50
#3: THE SECRET SANTA 87947-2/$3.50
#4: BAD DAY FOR BALLET 87948-0/$3.50
#5: THE SOCCER SHOE CLUE 87949-9/$3.50
#6: THE ICE CREAM SCOOP 87950-2/$3.50
#7: TROUBLE AT CAMP TREEHOUSE 87951-0/$3.99
#8: THE BEST DETECTIVE 87952-9/$3.50
#9: THE THANKSGIVING SURPRISE 52707-X/$3.50
#10: NOT NICE ON ICE 52711-8/$3.50
#11: THE PEN PAL PUZZLE 53550-1/$3.50
#12: THE PUPPY PROBLEM 53551-X/$3.50
#13: THE WEDDING GIFT GOOF 53552-8/$3.50
#14: THE FUNNY FACE FIGHT 53553-6/$3.50
#15: THE CRAZY KEY CLUE 56859-0/$3.50
#16: THE SKI SLOPE MYSTERY 56860-4/$3.50

by Carolyn Keene
Illustrated by Anthony Accardo

A MINSTREL® BOOK

Published by Pocket Books

Simon & Schuster Mail Order Dept. BWB
200 Old Tappan Rd., Old Tappan, N.J. 07675

Please send me the books I have checked above. I am enclosing $_____(please add $0.75 to cover the
postage and handling for each order. Please add appropriate sales tax). Send check or money order--no cash
or C.O.D.'s please. Allow up to six weeks for delivery. For purchase over $10.00 you may use VISA: card
number, expiration date and customer signature must be included.

Name _____

Address _____

City _____ State/Zip _____

VISA Card # _____ Exp.Date _____

Signature _____ 1045-10

FULL HOUSE™
Michelle

#1: THE GREAT PET PROJECT 51905-0/$3.50

#2: THE SUPER-DUPER SLEEPOVER PARTY
51906-9/$3.50

#3: MY TWO BEST FRIENDS 52271-X/$3.50

#4: LUCKY, LUCKY DAY 52272-8/$3.50

#5: THE GHOST IN MY CLOSET 53573-0/$3.99

#6: BALLET SURPRISE 53574-9/$3.99

#7: MAJOR LEAGUE TROUBLE 53575-7/$3.50

#8: MY FOURTH-GRADE MESS 53576-5/$3.99

#9: BUNK 3, TEDDY, AND ME 56834-5/$3.50

#10: MY BEST FRIEND IS A MOVIE STAR!
(Super Edition) 56835-3/$3.50

#11: THE BIG TURKEY ESCAPE 56836-1/$3.50

#12: THE SUBSTITUTE TEACHER 00364-X/$3.50

A MINSTREL® BOOK

Published by Pocket Books

Simon & Schuster Mail Order Dept. BWB
200 Old Tappan Rd., Old Tappan, N.J. 07675

Please send me the books I have checked above. I am enclosing $_____ (please add $0.75 to cover the postage and handling for each order. Please add appropriate sales tax). Send check or money order--no cash or C.O.D.'s please. Allow up to six weeks for delivery. For purchase over $10.00 you may use VISA: card number, expiration date and customer signature must be included.

Name _____

Address _____

City _____ State/Zip _____

VISA Card # _____ Exp.Date _____

Signature _____

™ & © 1997 Warner Bros. All Rights Reserved.
1033-15

MEET THE NEWEST DETECTIVE ON THE BLOCK!

Meet Mr. Pin, a rock hopper penguin who can't stay out of trouble. With a taste for chocolate and a nose for clues, Mr. Pin and his sidekick Maggie tackle Chicago's toughest crime cases.

Mr. Pin: The Chocolate Files

The Mysterious Cases of Mr. Pin

The Spy Who Came North From the Pole: Mr. Pin Vol. III

by
MARY ELISE MONSELL

**Available from Minstrel® Books
Published by Pocket Books**

702-03

TAKE A RIDE
WITH THE KIDS ON BUS FIVE!

Natalie Adams and James Penny have just started
third grade. They like their teacher, and they like
Maple Street School. The only trouble is, they have
to ride bad old Bus Five to get there!

#1 THE BAD NEWS BULLY
Can Natalie and James stop the bully on Bus Five?

#2 WILD MAN AT THE WHEEL
When Mr. Balter calls in sick,
the kids get some strange new drivers.

#3 FINDERS KEEPERS
The kids on Bus Five keep losing things.
Is there a thief on board?

(And coming soon)
#4 I SURVIVED ON BUS FIVE
Bad luck turns into big fun
when Bus Five breaks down in a rainstorm.

BY MARCIA LEONARD
ILLUSTRATED BY JULIE DURRELL

A MINSTREL® BOOK

Published by Pocket Books

1237-03